Whale Bones

Muddy D Norman

Acknowledgments

All poems in this book have been curated by M Hawk

Front cover design by Veronica Carrara

Cover Photo Annette Shaff

Seabhac

© 2019 Muddy D Norman

All rights reserved.

ISBN: 9781090413581

For My Son

Oisin O Laoghaire

Contents

In conversation with the poet /7
Introduction by M Hawk /12

Desire:
That place /15
Two songs for my muse:
Forward memory / I know her name /16
Young eye /19
Dreams again /20
Remembering /21
You /22
The dance /23
First kiss /24
Elegy for a dream /25
Shrine /26

Antipathy:
Anthem /28
Not enough /30
The season of the witch /31
How love died /32
On moth wings /33
Long past love /34

Solitude
Not now /36
Night walker /37
Time /38
A prayer for my son /39
Asylum road /40
Old /41

Shadows:
Landscape /43
Written in long hand /44
Three sister's sanatorium /45
Night /48
Infirmary /49
The long wait /58

Gods & Monsters
Ballad of a self-made man /62
Creation myth /63
Muriwai's diving bird /64
Whale bones /66
From Gethsemane to Golgotha /67
The last of the coven /69
A war of composition /71
The season of the wolf /73

The Fallen
When we were gods /76
Black Jack's well /77
Alienation /78
The lunatic /79
Joy rider /81
Burning bridges /82

IN CONVERSATION WITH THE POET

The following interview took place between Mel Hawk and Muddy D Norman in August 2019.

MH: How did you come to write poetry?

MDN: I left school in 1981/82, unable to read or write because I am dyslexic. I went to sea as a deckhand and it was while I was at sea that I taught myself to read and write by transcribing books that were on board. At the time mostly westerns or erotic novels. When I got home I transcribed whatever books were lying around, mostly poetry books belonging to my dad.

I loved poetry books, initially because I could transcribe them much quicker than novels, which made me feel like I was achieving something. A bonus was that I came across new words more often in poetry. I came across strange syntax and unusual placement of words, their meaning stretched to their limits. The meaning was not always apparent and had to be searched for. I learned more from poetry than anything else.

I transcribed poetry books to learn to write. When I ran out of poetry books to transcribe I just wrote my own; it helped me make sense of the world.

It's where I learned everything I know. It's where I make sense of or at least try to understand or come to terms with the things that choke you with fear. Like death and loss. It's where you learn about the things that fill you with happiness.

Poetry is where the demons live and where the angels make love, where you learn about yourself and others, either by dissecting them in poems or through their reactions to your poetry or the fact that you write at all.

MH: What does poetry mean to you?

MDN: I have lost a lot of friends over the years to poetry and made quite a few new ones. Some I lost were offended by a word I'd used or even a few who thought I was being pretentious because I wrote poetry. Writing poetry to me now is a compulsion, it's a habit, but more than that, it is my great joy!

All those long nights sitting at my desk scribbling away, writing line after line, inspired by something tiny, a word I heard while speaking to someone, just shooting the breeze and they utter a phrase or a single word and that's all I need to start a poem. I could be at it for weeks writing rewriting and reworking a single poem, that's where the joy is, in the writing of it. The rest is a pain in the ass.

MH: Where did the title Whale Bones come from?

MDN: The poem Infirmary was initially called whale bones but I cut a few stanzas from it and suddenly the title made no sense but I liked it for the title of the book, as several poems contain the phrase.

Whale Bones; it conjures for me a very bleak and desolate image. It conjures up a cold and empty place an endless desert or beach with no features. This was what the poem infirmary was about, the isolation and loneliness of PTSD.

While I was in the Coast Guard, I suffered from post-traumatic stress which manifested itself as anaphylaxis. So I'd be rushed to hospital where they would inject me with steroids and antihistamine. Then do a shitload of tests and find nothing!

So they sent me to a psychiatrist and she diagnosed me with PTSD and sent me to a psychologist who tried to convince me that my illness was mental and not physical. It was physical but manifested by a mental health issue

(PTSD) I was a medical marvel.

It took some time to convince me that my illness couldn't be cured by medicine only cognitive therapy and counseling, which was a very terrifying and painful experience.

In the poem infirmary, the nurse takes on the part of the illness. So in a sense, the poem is about clinging to the comfort of the illness, I imagine that's what hypochondria or Munchausen's to be like, a co-dependent relationship.

The poem three sisters sanatorium is about the cure, a dreadful experience, well it was for me! But, in hindsight, it was an amazing thing.

MH: Was the PTSD the result of one particular incident or was it the accumulation of a lifetime of trauma?
MDN: The PTSD came from a lifetime of trauma as you suggested. My first memory is of my father performing CPR on my brother who had whooping cough. My second memory was digging his grave and then his funeral. After that my mother became very depressed, my father went the other direction became very affectionate and loving. If it wasn't for him life would have been unbearable.

Then there was the coast guard but that's another story.

MH: What do you think are the main themes that run through this book?
MDN: I think most of the poems in this book are about love and death, what else is there? I think that the answers to all life's problems can be found in love, and if not there, then death will have the answers. Most of the poems are about the transition from life into death, either the start of a love affair or the end of one. I don't know if I managed to convey this in the poems themselves, but no matter, that is an issue for the reader. The

poems are about the start of things and the end of things regardless of what those things are. The beginning and the end of a loving relationship or a torrid affair are the most interesting.

MH: Is writing a form of therapy for you?

MDN: I don't think that you can write your way out of that shit! While I was in therapy the last thing I could do was write. It's a very traumatic experience that cuts away all the flesh and leaves you exposed in a way that no human should ever be. The cure is always worse than the disease; however, it is that experience that fuels the writing.

You can't get away from it, it is a constant. Even though I have been cured my writing will always have elements of that experience in it. My writing is completely immersed in that experience and always will be. It is part of the language of my life. I know nothing else, I write from my experience and my experience is my life.

MH: Who were the poets that inspired you?

MND: My dad wrote poems. When I was a kid I remember the house being covered in scraps of paper with his poems written on them. He was a commie and an Irish nationalist he was very interested in the Maori land march and the whole Bastion Point saga in New Zealand in the '70s and '80s that is how he first came to know Hone Tuwhare's poetry. The greatest thing my father gave me was a photocopy of one of his books Sapwood and Milk; my dad liked Tuwhare because he fought the British Empire. He gave me Hone's book when he saw me transcribe poetry books, I lost it somewhere along the way. The same with my father's poems, I only have a few left.

So that was my introduction to modern poets. My father introduced me to the Kiwi poets Tuwhare and Baxter. I later discovered Sam Hunt and Bob Orr.

Durcan was the first modern Irish poet that I read. A friend gave me a copy of The Berlin Wall Café. It was the first book of poetry that I read where I could hear the poet's voice. Durcan was like Bukowski to me. I later found the same thing with Theo Dorgan; the voice was always there; you can almost hear his accent when you read his poems. Theo Dorgan has a way of infusing an atmosphere in his work, I think that is the most important element in poetry it's the atmosphere, more so than rhyme, rhythm or syntax. Most of my favorite poems have an atmosphere or at least invoke a feeling from somewhere inside.

INTRODUCTION

It is no easy task to write an introduction to this collection of works. Over recent months I have spent a lot of time with these poems. I have read them in my head and out loud to feel the difference when words are made real by speaking them.

I have considered them, critiqued them, have come to know them by name. Some of the lines have worked their way into my soul and, quite by accident, I have memorized them

There is value in remembering the past and putting it in some kind of order. Muddy D Norman is a collector of moments and experiences. MDN enters where angels fear to tread to capture on the page heartfelt longing and the dark night of the soul.

The powerful imagery of deserted landscapes, the lament for lost innocence and melancholic solitude are tempered by the call to love, to see beauty in the ordinary and to remember there is humour in our earthbound predicament

MDN writes from a raw and unashamedly personal place. Sometimes these poems confront, sometimes they offer solace and wisdom of one who has faced his demons, corralled them into words and committed them to paper. Sometimes these poems elicit a smile and a memory. They are always searching for meaning and seeking the truth.

I have approached these poems on different days, through different seasons, at different points in time. Some speak loudly, some shout, some provoke and some resonate over time. Others stand outside patiently and offer an occasional soft knock. Let them in.

M Hawk

DESIRE

That place

There is a place where I've never been
But in dreams kissed
Its wet shoreline
And slept on its golden ground
Woke to the smell of falling petals
That wash me clean

Two songs for my muse

1

Forward memory

I knew her
Long before the high summer sun
Scorched across the sky
I remembered her when I was young
Long before I met her

I remembered her with gorse popping blooms
On that march I made home from the Atlantic
When the marrow was young
And the spirit soared with the swallows
On the high hot thermals
I felt her touch then
In the heather scratched ankles
And the blistering
Nettle stung wrapped
In doc leaf fingers

I knew her name
Before words could describe it
Words as cold water
On a parched tongue
Nectar sucked from a fuchsia

Bitter sorrel picked from beneath
A cemetery wall

I remember her now
In old age
Not the contours of her face
Or the sound of her name
But my mouth remembers the shape of it
And the shape of her kiss

2
I know her name

It left no trace before she came
I memorized it like a song
Utter it only to the still silence
Reluctantly
For fear it might escape me

I know her name
Never far from my tongue
A Eucharist-
Stuck to the roof of my mouth
I sing it as a hymn to the god of her

I know her name
Mutter it only in whispers
Murmur it only in soft prayers-
It forms shapes in my mouth
Soft shapes of Celtic knots
Its Cockle shell sharp loops
And twists

When I speak it spirals off my tongue
It oscillates slowly
Tasting its frequencies
Savoring it

Young eye

I need to look through young eyes again
Through this winter's grey veil
Back to autumnal amber skies-
Shed experience and walk for the first time on dew cold grass
That the blue light of a summer dawn has not yet touched-
And brush aside the golden strands of hair that touch your face-
Kiss pale pink lips and inhale sweet coffee and nicotine breath

Dreams again

I dreamt of whalebones again last night
You beached between the sheets
Lost in dreams of better men
Whalebones cling to your ribs
Laced to your shoulder blades
Sharp
Cutting muscle
Shaping skin-
A cursed rose tattoo that strangles me
This foul and demented me

Remembering

There was a time
When I could tell if the moon
Was in wax or wane
I could name every constellation
And every constituent star-
I could wish on every one
On this
Start light
Star bright night
Wishing I could
Wishing I might
Instead I join each star point to point
Drawing your face across the sky

You

I picked you flowers
Rhododendrons I think
But the petals fell from the stem
Before I got them home

I try sweetheart
I really do
But I can't seem to get to the end of anything

I tried staying in love with you
But you made it so hard
With your
Endless smile
And incessant joy

The dance

She danced with the passion of Salome

Under a rain silver sky

She scarred my heart

Scrawled her name across it

With her sickle foot

Adagio

Hell raising flamenco

Her wet skin reflected candle light

My blood raced to the beat of her castanets

I ached to the vision of her fishnets

Ill cut the head off any man

And serve it on a salver

First kiss

It rained the day we met

Just like it did when Mars met Venus

Boughs bent heavy

With the wind

The green pacific

Curled its tongue like waves

Beneath the Christmas trees

In the glare of street lights

Out there by the three sea monsters

Where you danced along the promenade

Arms out stretched

Singing with the rain

And all the while

Filling me with a madness

A dark madness of possession

You howled at the peeking moon

I became close-fisted envious

Of its gain

How it captured your attention

Love is a lonely place

Crowded as it is with lovers and losers

I never wanted it more than then

The rain

The sea monsters

The Christmas trees

Elegy for a dream

 I will write for those

Who dream of the strangest worlds

Of angels forever in the mist

A shamans lost soul

Carried away

By a naked witch

Day dreams of lost wishes

That tip toe

In soft shoes

Through the blackest nights

The pool craving

A love ocean deep-

Making waves that return as regret

Shrine

(for Izabella Malcer)

We cultivated our garden at night
Treading softly on the lawn
Whispering over the cicadas hum
Surrounded by your sea shells
Collected on your pilgrimages

In dreams
Always in dreams
You at the water's edge
Walking with clean feet and solemn gait
Under a soft moon
Choosing jeweled relics for your alter

ANTIPATHY

Anthem

Your undying love
My mourning dove

Your empty conscience
My incriminating correspondence

Your matter of fact
My deviant act

Your accusation
My counter allegation

Your interrogation
My admission

Your aggression
My confession

Your battleground
My weeping wound

Your eyes are black
My knuckles cracked

Your temper tantrum
My fighting bantam

Your five minute contraction
My knee jerk reaction

Your stigmata
My persona non grata

Your gin and tonic
My plague bubonic

You had to involve her
I absolved her

Your walk away
My wave good day

Not enough

There should have been more than this
Black butterfly's
Gossamer wings tangled
On your net curtains
Carried its omens from the pupas
Brought the end of all the little things

A black butterfly
Casts a flickering shadow over
Your corroded soul
That lies scattered on your laminate floor
Guts tight full of butterflies

The season of the witch

Overseer of the firmament
Magician of the flesh
Around her alter naked she flies
Screaming solemn incantations
The darkened night retorts with fits of thunder!
Fairies around the dolmen dance
To the rhythm of her chants
The woods alight with demon sprite
And the ghosts of long dead knights
Cavort with vampire hermaphrodites
Through her bonfire flames she dances
One hand on her round ripe breast
The other grippes a poppet
An effigy of an enemy an unrighteous man
A brigand and a treacherous knave
Who broke his solemn vow
Above the thunderous storms
She screams angry invocations
That echo through the trees
The poppet gripped between her teeth
In both hands flaming torches
Death is on her lips

How love died

Love died on a stained mattress
Wrapped in dirty sheets

Blue murder she cried
Finger pointed accusation
A slapped cheek betrayal
No alibi
No provision for insanity

The suspect dejected
Police cordon erected
Broken crockery chalk out lined
Sharpened cutlery dusted
Foul play suspected
All the evidence collected

Its murder she cried
But that's not how love died
It was a little petit mort
By a little miss adventure

On moths' wings

Her lies counted on the fingers of one hand
The truth on one finger of the other-

It's a malediction to remember
The low tide smell of her pussy
A basilica for low men forever pillaged
And plundered
Promises just like
Moth wings burn in a candles flame

Long past love

A cyst on her womb is what she called me
Her little ball bag buffoon
I make jack hammer love to her
And when I'm done
She rolls over
Rolls her eyes to heaven
Makes no attempt to hide
The bored look on her face
But at least there is no contempt
At least not yet
We are long past love

We are singing our requiem
She still laughs when I cry
We became bad habits
Found comfort in our strangeness
We are each other's old slippers
We are long past love

SOLITUDE

Not now

Now is not the time
Down here among the whale bones
To take captive her heart-

It isn't now
Among the empty shells
Feathers shed by dead gulls
Down here among the flotsam
And dried sea foam
Down here among
The washed-up jetsam
Blue skies
Tricks of the light
Trickery of eyesight

Now is not the time
Down here among the needs a mop lino
The morning after lovers
The sink stacked dishes
The mound of butt stuffed beer cans
The twice used dry tea bags

Leave her heart where it is
High above the high-water mark
High above the whale bones

Night walker

I walked the rain wet
Railway tracks
Following the moon lit rails
Trying to weave poems out of memories
Trying to tread through rhyme and rhythm

Passing orchards of crab apples
Where a choir of nightingales
Whistle the stars across the sky
Stop only to listen to the
Bursting applause
Of a wood pigeon taking flight

Time

She stands alone
The retreating second hand
Reclaims lost seconds
The bell un-rings
The cuckoo spellbound
Frozen in mid flight
Silent
The pendulum still
The wise alone awake
While everyone sleeps
In dreams river deep

A prayer to my son

When your heart beats
It marks in transition
Time
The seconds fall

Hours turn to years

When your heart beats
It attends to the rhythm of your breath
Your dreams
Paint images
Impasto on your mind
Bright holograms
That lights the cold darkness

Easy now
For tomorrow brings its sun
With the sun more seasons
And in their turn seasons
Fall to
Forever and ever
Time is now your greatest friend
But will turn unstoppable like the tide
Into your greatest enemy

Asylum road

I can't tell when it's twisted
This road I'm on
The destination I've forgotten
God knows where I started from
I just follow it now
This melt down macadam
This river of asphalt
This tar terra firma

I can't tell if it deviates
Or if my mind is deflected
Put the sign posts
Read rewind
The rear view mirror
Reveals the last exit
For last Minute Pass

I can't tell where it's going
This road I'm on
But if you silence the long road
And draw a curtain of cloud across the headlight moon
I'll be home to sleep quietly beside you

Old

When I'm an old and angry drunk
When all I have is empty wine bottles and other peoples butts to smoke
Who will love me then?

Who will shower me in temper tantrums?
Whose wagging nagging tongue
Will remind me of my wasted life?

We were gods once
Genesis was ours
We were everything to each other
What gods we were

Shadows

Landscape

I wanted to paint a picture
Black basalt painting
Of an iron sand beach
With a Prussian blue sea
And sliver moon
I would have painted it all gull quiet
Wet periwinkle rocks
Breaking waves

I would have painted ghosts on the sand
That smelled of white spirits
And in the distance before the coast gets all jagged
I'll paint a man
Me
Dragging your body across
The moon lit sand
Off to drown my sorrows
A sort of exorcism.

Written in long hand

Released from a poet's prism
Freed from ropes
Of rhyme and rhythm
No more hourglasses
No more falling sand
One last midnight
A dialect angles can't understand
Letters from a dead man
Written with a trembling hand
One last daybreak
Suckling a mammary gland
A last cigarette
And last words scrawled on paper
A letter from a dead man's hand

Three sister's sanatorium (Resurrection song)

I

The siren sound

The creeping search light in full bloom

Kept me awake last night

Evicted from my Iron lung

Pulled from corners of that room

Pulled butterflies from the womb

Eyes frost white and

Frost bite blue

Sold my soul for solitude

II

I imagine stone cut gargoyles

Sneers chiseled granite stiff

Viper tongued and bat winged

Hanging over grey metal beds

Frightening the nearly dead

Did I forsake you?

A hand full of false idol

Beating the bishop

III

I have left my iron lung

Lead shoes and dead legs prevent my run

I shuffle chain gang down the hall

A slack line draped over

An un-balanced moon

A crazed rat

Running from a tom cat

Crawling through the wreckage of a fallen star

Brought down by the weight of wishes

IV

I am to be shrink wrapped

I talked myself into it

There is no talking myself out of it

They will sanitize my mind

I hope they leave something behind

A little something behind the eyes

V

The clouds break

Giving me an up skirt view

Of the camel toed moon

I'm in traction

Rigged to this contraption

This is my act of contrition

Electrodes stuck to my cranium

I am to be traumatized

Into tranquility

The jolting amps conduct St Vitas dance

VI

Three days have come and gone

Three nights of fit full

Feverish sleep

Lost to the ether

My morning bird has turned to an old crow

A mourning bird

VII

My Hystericalectomy was a great success

I am to be released back into the wild

Back out of my fucking mind

Back into a living womb

I stand blinking in the sun light

My kit bag packed with oddments

And trepanation tools

Night

On this

The Shortest night

The moths mistake my candle for the moon

I watch

As they burn

In silence

I sit

Orphaned

Infirmary (Departure day)

Her sour tongue
Rasped its way into my mouth
I have tasted her yeast infection
And saw the skin crack at the corner of her smile
My pretty nunnery nurse
My bitter postulant

She walks on narwhal tusks
Her hair throws Great bird wing shadows on the wall
She is my morning bird

Day two

My blood in doldrums
Capillary action soaks bandages red
Those foul-smelling rags need to be changed
She pours Iodine over the dressings
Staining the skin
Runs nicotine to the sheets
The only joy is to glimpse her pendulous breasts
Before they caress my cheek
As she leans to tuck me in

Day three

A Late evening
Late spring
Fever leaves me close to combustion
Our falling star turns the gray walls orange
A lawnmower purrs
The sound of a poor bastard beast laboring in the fields
If I only had the strength to make it to the window
Before the heavy antiseptic air sends me to sleep

Day four

Here she comes again my morning bird
Gripped in her soft surgical gloved hands
Her stainless-steel kidney dish
Full of sharp scalpels
And ointments
Bitter remedies
For all my maladies
She smells of sex and anger
I smell of piss and despair

Day five

I catch a scent of the sea
Or at least salt on the air
I can't feel the pull of the tide
It's too faint
Heart beat faint
If I could make it to the window
I could watch the sun die slowly

Great news
I'm down to my ideal weight

Day six

Ill shit diamonds when dignity dies
I need cold porcelain
For my cheeks
Someone left during the night
Whispers in the dark
Porter's moaning under the dead weight
Matron wrapped his effects in brown paper
I could hear her arthritic fingers creek and groan
Like a clipper taking heavy seas
Before morning a new one arrives
The bed never goes cold

Day seven

Soft boiled eggs
Warm
Salted
Burst like an abscess
The old priest saves souls
With teeth pulling effort
Wipes sin from the corner of his mouth

My morning bird arrives again
Carries with her the stench of bed pans
The tragedy of man
Is just the comedy of Pan

Day eight

Am I a fucking exhibit or am I a miracle?
Is my bed a crushed velvet covered plinth?
Is the chart that hangs at the foot of my bed a brass plaque?
"Here lie the wounded
Don't look them in the eye
You'll get infected"

Day nine

My balls blue from the unction
My piss green
My skin ghost gray
My morning bird
Is turning me into a human kaleidoscope
Stabbed with an intravenous marlin spike
Blood sugar that once rushed
Now seeps
Her moustache scratched my cheek
As she whispered in my ear
"We will have no more talk of miracles"

Our sick bed soviet
Lost another last night
I never knew his name
But Cerberus guarded his bed

Day ten

My mourning dove
My pterodactyl love
Changed my bandages at last
Her talons ripped the skin
Took scabs an'all
Replaced them with a bastard toad flax poultice
Her beak stung my lips as we kissed
This is not making love
Her breath stinks of cock and gin
Her beauty lost to me now
Under blankets
Under pain
I see beneath her skin
Her red rib cage
Held together with a whalebone corset

I swear to Christ
I can feel the maggot
Squirm beneath my fresh bandages
I can feel them bite my
Rotten flesh
She put them there
A mother bird feeding her young
My love bird my Valkyrie
After my bones

Day eleven

The gray priest
Anointed the dead with sunflower oil
The next dead
In the next bed
Withdrew his medication
Not fit for resuscitation
He sang last night in his delirium
Something about storm petrels
That dance in the wind
I screamed "Just die you fucker, die!"
We both cried softly until we slept
He passed by morning
Left only his confession
And his sour grapes
The priest marked the sign of the cross on his forehead

You know we never eat the grapes you bring
When have you ever seen us eat grapes?

Day does it really matter

Lost count
Lost consequence
Heels dug into soft sand
Rose quartz clutched in my hand
Still I slide down hill

I swear to god
I can feel the maggots
Squirm beneath the compress

Day who cares
We are all soldiers here
Wounded there
Pitied everywhere
In a fallacy of judgment
We are turned
Into refugees

The blind bulbs give no light
The seeing bring soft borders to the shadows
Blink Christmassy
Sick taste on my tongue
Bleach burns my nostrils
I cling to the wreckage of hope
Slowly drowning

I hear the maggots talking
About blood slowing
My dressings rise and fall
Breathing a life of their own

Here she comes
My little shroud seamstress
Like an air licking lizard
Hunting with a flicking tongue
My miasma shrouded carcass
With her curved asp snakebite
And her mercury cure all
Her syringes full of
Mrs. Winslow's soothing syrup
She leaves me chewing burnt matches

There are no wounds here
Malingerer
Flincher
Cringer
Departure day is here!

The long wait

My dealing death where have you been
What relics did you bring to tempt me?
When I was young I feared you
I trembled in your shadow

But now you are just a messenger
Life's last narrator
Your gift
A blessed relief
A long-lasting sleep
I burn my candle to light your weary way-

Oh death my friend
I thought I'd never see you
Forgotten you'd return it seems
But the nurse knew you'd visit soon
And kept the bedside clean-

Old friend sit for a while with me and let me reminisce.
Of how she made me laugh and cry
That green-eyed temptress

Don't worry my old friend I won't beg or plead-
Just watch one last sun set with me and
Have one for the road
Share my last cigarette
And we'll sing the moon awake

Sit awhile my friend and let me fall asleep
Take my hand in your hand and whisper in my ear
"Don't be afraid old man it's time to go
And leave this place to tomorrow's young"

Gods & Monsters

The ballad of a self-made man

I was born unfinished
A fragmented half-baked boy
Rewired and electrified
The turned around brain
Knitting a nexus of synapses
To hide memories in
Cut hands from granite
Carved deep lines across the palm
Knotted cat gut from tip of finger to wrist
Making bow taut sinews
That will never lose their grip

The nails I cut from cataracts
The eyes I carved from coal
Used broken beer bottles
For the glint
Fashioned lashes from spider's legs
Made brows from their little webs
Wove a beard from a wolf cur's matted fur

Made limbs out of trunk and branch
Turned marrow to blood
Burrowed with vein and arteries
Through flesh wrapped around bough bones

I cut myself a heart from old shoe leather
Soaked it in paraffin
I keep it in an old ribcage
Made from a lobster pot
All of this I wrapped tightly
In fine down covered cellophane skin
At night under dim candle light
I confront the bully within
Trying to sculpt a knave into a king

Creation myth

The coast gave birth to Venus
Cast in its imaginings
Golden hair and silver skin-
From her mouth fell rain
Creating rivers
Birthed from high hill wombs
Mist covered home for frog hunting herons
Carves banks on its rush
To its lowest point
On its way sculpts
Salmon leaps from rock
Dark reed filled pools for trout to hide from fly fishers
Like a vein running back to the heart
Filling oceans
From her lotus bud
She bled
Thighs run red
Salting all the water
Creating mortal lovers
Filling their days with melancholy
And their nights with fevered desire
Pulling from summer autumn
Conducted the rag worms
Mating dance
Filling estuaries with flounder

Muriwai's diving bird

Perfection in the geometry of her face
Left him breathless
And still
Captive to his imagination
Adrift in his own genesis

She her own god
Poised for movement
Paused for breath
As wild as wild can be
Dived into the Tasman Sea

Gliding with the king fish
Over constellations of star fish
Orbiting an urchin moon
Riding the undertows
Beneath the seething waves
Creates herself in her own image
Remembers herself as a laughing bird
A sacred thing
Wild as wild can be
Wilder than the Tasman Sea.

He stands alone

A lost god on the shore

Full of fury and faithless

As mad as mad can be

Madder than

Kupe singing to the wild sea

Whale bones

On bone Kupe carved his history
Drawing blood as he sang his rage into the shape of it

Cut whale bone harpoons
To catch an apparition
On a shoreline of phantoms

Rough hued his fight with sea monsters
Still singing his rage
His furious storm song
That boiled the sea
Boiled it mad
Overturning
Charging war canoes

At sunset
He stood in foaming surf
Always in his hand
His greenstone club
Polished by hands and time
Reviling a captured sky

From Gethsemane to Golgotha

Arcadia cannot fall if it hasn't risen
The dirt poor collecting handouts for the filthy rich
The latest coronation the ascension of clowns under a golden crown
Democracies run by the aristocracy
For the glitterati and their cliterati wives
All reprobates masturbating over the master race

This pass through the universe
Has left Nobody burdened with love
Weighed down Nobody with longing
Nobody bought all they were selling
Hypocrisy by the pound
The depleted coffers used as coffins

In this garden Nobody wallows in self-pity
Adoring false profits
Petitioning dead deities
With deceitful bargaining prayers
Suffering through a famine of morality
While they feast on weapons grade dishonesty

With blasting trumpets
And whore Termagants singing
They lead him up Golgotha
The bull shitters leading nobody
Signing braille contracts with blood

The Romans in their coliseum

Feed him to the Christians

And he danced and he skipped

To his DIY crucifixion

Nobody can stop empires from falling

The last of the coven

'Ah!' she cried the night she died
Her voice full of fear and doubt

'Ah!' she cried the night she died
But no one was there to attend her

'Don't be fooled' she cried
'The moon is always full'

Her dead cat looked familiar
And replied "It's always fucking raining"

'And the sun is always shining'
But no one was there to take any heed
.
Her wisdom like her dreams
Gravitate to the floor

Just dust in a shaft of sunlight
'Ah!' she cried as the dead arrived

And shuffled in to greet her
Her cauldron cold covered in mould

Her little things surround her
Her tinctures of nail polish

Combs and emery boards
 The perfumed potions

And soft skin lotions
'Where's Hades?' she cried

The dead replied "He's indisposed repossessing souls'
'What about mine?' she cried

'It's worth its weight in gold' she lied
The dead, the dead gathered round her bed

And chanted incantations
Her soul it raised its weary head

And staggered from the bed
At last she's dead

A war of composition

The nine daughters of Zeus

Lie in ambush

Waiting for Hypnos to cast his spell

And just as I melt into sleep

They trip their trigger

At first just a word

Whispered into the ear

A word that floats across the mind's eye

Grabbing the attention

Evoking blurred faces

Forgotten names

Waking my curiosity stirring my imagination-

Hop scotching across memories

The battleground chosen

Now they really come

The little demonic bastards –

I wrestle them

Pull them apart

Reshape them

Hold them hostage

Discard them

Summarily execute them

The battle writhes to and fro

Sometimes succumbing

To their brutal beauty

The succubus of song and rhyme-

More often
I succeed in forcing them to my will.
Over powering them
I make them confess to their meaning
Make them say what I want
Arrange and rearrange
Until they say it the way I want
And it goes on

All night the skirmishing with words
Grappling ideas into coherent meaning
On it goes past the dawn
Well into the day
When finally victory is declared

The rolled-up paper corpse of the dead litter no man's land
Butts fill the ashtray like spent shells
The battle report dispatched.
I crawl into the sheets
Weary with fatigue
Fit only for
Dreamless sleep
In victorious defeat
All I have won
Is a few short verses
That no one will ever read

The season of the wolf

I am all that is —
I am the Id
I am the halo of the moon
I am the end of time
The light of the furthest star

I am the eater of slow rabbits
The stalker of lame deer
I am the ransom of all kings
I am all and all is mine

I am hunter
Shaman
Priest
I hide in the shadow of the soothsayer
I whisper in his ear

I am the feast that tempts you
The curve of her ripe breast
I am the stray dog in the rain
I know where your cats lie slain

I am the howl of madness
That makes you beg forgiveness
I am the cold breath on your neck
That shivers down your spine

I am footsteps following

The long claw scratching

The rabid tongue licking

I am all that is

The final retribution

The holy visitation

Your eternal damnation

I am the godless one

Vengeance incarnate

I hunt by the dark of night

I am the light that loves the shadows

The dark that preys on fear

I am he that was not born

And he that will not die

I am all you fear

The Fallen

When we were gods

Before the quickening days of age
Before wisdom had lost us the will to action
Or we
Not yet prudent enough to let the zealous youth take point-
In human fallibility we forced life to bend and twist
Creating with unsettled minds an unsettled life-

Let the youth rage and fight an un-seen enemy
Leave them to their fleeting victory dances
And their melancholy doldrums of defeat
Let them fill their days with turbulence and fuss
Blustering nights full of lighting and thunder
What need has youth for wisdom?
When it has the power of muscle
Sinew and strong-willed stamina

When their laborious work is done
When they are walking
Stooped on bending sticks
Mad with unspent lust
At their low tide
When the falling sun
Has left them with long shadows
When their eyes have dimmed
And age withers the ego
That is when god dies

Black Jack's well

He passed through the garden
Gorged himself on apples
Feasted on innocence
Now it is his to toil
Fatigue into
Restless sleep
Full of unnerving dreams
Gave up the suckling breast
Took up knife and fork
Laboured long to dig his deep well

But hold your tongue
Unflair your nostrils
Remember the old days
When gods were worriers
And whores priestess's
When a poet's tongue
Howled like vagabond dogs

Hauld yer Whisht
Keep your wives tails between your legs
No one wants to hear judgment from the Aspidistras.

Alienation

National socialist chauvinists
Wage war on the clitoris
While academic feminists
Wage war for middle management wages

Pillaged and broke
Bigotry is a pope with a rope
Filling paradise with paedos

Transient transsexuals
Board trains that never leave the station
Divided and conquered
Pillaged and painted
Wage war for real men

The lunatic

The lunatic is chasing useless things again
Following with blood shot eyes
Non-existent dive-bombing flies

He is chasing useless things again
Long legs in short skirts
Halfcocked red lipstick smiles
That makes him climb
The bending stairs to his cobwebbed
Dead mouse attic mind

He rummages among the useless things
Through the cinders of old flames
Cremated promises that smoldered out
His fingers rake through the cold black ashes
Of sacrificial ejaculations
That lie on altars of some
Goddess or other
Just sins he cast out
Magick spells he shed in a rain of tears

The lunatic is chasing useless things again

Wild things

Savage things

Collecting pain

To make a talisman

A shapeless amulet

A madstone

For trickery and treason

The lunatic is chasing useless things again

Crazy useless things

Joy rider

Living on his accelerator
Braking only for burnouts
Scorched tire aftershave
Beating pistons
Beating cardiac combustion
Listening to the melody
Of Velcro tyres
Ripping off the black macadam

Burning bridges

My arson's match strikes keen-
Sparks fear-
Sulphur stings the nostrils-
Adrenalin shakes the fingers
The smoldering fuse fizzes
Races with the heart to ignition
Flash and boom of detonation –
Mushroom cloud of acrid smoke-
Burn all my bridges brightly –
A pyre for past indiscretion
Sinner or sinned against
Burn them like beacons
Fair warning -
No one can follow
And when
I stumble over doubt
No retreat for me
Turn my back on the orange glow of conflagration
Consternation and confession-
A firestorm of retribution -
Let it light my way
To the next bridge to burn

Printed in Poland
by Amazon Fulfillment
Poland Sp. z o.o., Wrocław